CHILDREN OF THE FUTURE

JANE SUEN

Jane Suen LLC Books are available for order through Ingram Press Catalogues

www.janesuen.com

Printed in the United States of America

First Printing: August 2016

ISBN: 978-0-9979297-0-6
Ebook ISBN: 978-0-9979297-1-3

For my mother and father, always.

CHILDREN OF
THE FUTURE

Chapter 1

MONDAY

"I'll see you after school!" Telly shouted above the noise of the engine as he pulled the door closed. Little did he know that today would be different.

He drove the yellow school bus from the small, red brick Rocky Flats Elementary School to the bus yard and parked. He switched vehicles, got in his beat-up blue pickup, and drove to his second job at the cabinet shop.

Stretching his long legs as he swiveled out of his seat, Telly extended the full length of his 6-foot-4 frame until his boots touched the ground. As he turned around and took off his sunglasses, he glimpsed his face in the rear-view mirror as he reached over to put them on the dashboard. Pleased, Telly ran his fingers over his thick sandy hair. His thick head of hair framed a rugged face ... a strong jaw line.

Working in the shop, absorbed in the hum and rhythm of sanding wood, his mind and body were focused and in sync, not missing a beat. Telly quickly lost track of time. Before he knew it, the day had flown by. Telly realized in a panic that he was going to be late picking up the kids at school. He whipped off his safety goggles and dust mask, brushed the sawdust off his t-shirt and jeans, and stomped his boots to shake off the wood shavings. He rushed out, hating to be late. He cursed under his breath. He'd never been late picking up the kids. Telly prided himself for being on time, especially on this job as the bus driver. None of the kids should ever have to wait on him.

He dropped off his truck at the bus yard and drove the bus as fast as he dared. Pulling up in front of the school, he was relieved when he didn't see any kids in the schoolyard. He thought he had made it just in time. But, after he sat and waited, Telly began to think something was out of place. The bell should have rung at 2:30 p.m., and the doors should have opened.

He checked his watch. It seemed to be working fine. It was 2:34 p.m.... but there was still no sign of any kids.

Telly's mind raced, trying to make sense of it. He was not supposed to leave the school bus until all the kids were on it; but, by this time there was no telling how much longer he would have to wait. His eyes searched the school, finally resting on the front door. *To heck with it!* Telly made a quick decision. Grasping the handle, he pushed open the bus door.

As Telly rushed out of his bus to look around, his anger evaporated. A chill filled him, tightening its grip around his heart. He tried to shake it off, but with a sinking feeling, he felt it expand, right down to the pit of his stomach.

The school was strangely quiet, nothing, not a sound. He opened the front door. He heard nothing. There was no sign on the door, and no sign of any kids. Telly went to the principal's office to see if anyone was there. Empty. He peeked in the classrooms. Empty. He walked the halls. The only sound he heard was the *clump-clump* of his boots on the wooden floors. He looked in the schoolyard. Empty. *Where is everyone?*

Chapter 2

FRIDAY, 3 DAYS EARLIER

It was a sunny day. The school bus pulled up and Billy moved forward. The driver opened the door, smiled, and said, "Hey Billy, how's it going?" It was Friday morning and a good start to the day, Telly thought, as he closed the door and drove through the countryside. He stopped the bus a few more times to pick up Ron, Liz, Annie, and Bryan before heading into the small town of Rocky Flats. Telly liked to watch the people buzzing about on their way to wherever they had to go. He wondered where they were going, what they would do with their day. The kids on the bus were chatting and laughing. All in all, just another day like any other, and a beautiful day. He loved his job, all of it.

Pulling up in front of the school, Telly opened the door and said good-bye to the kids as they left. He watched as they disembarked, one by one. The time was 7:50 a.m. Telly stayed there a moment after all the kids were safely off, watching as the last kid disappeared inside Rocky Flats Elementary School. Telly had a second job to go to until it was time to pick up the kids in the afternoon. He drove the bus to the bus yard to make a switch, then drove his truck to his part-time job at the cabinet shop.

"How's it going, Telly?" Ray shouted across the room, as he walked in.

"Hey, man, doing ok!" Telly shouted back as he pulled on his work gloves and got started. The project that he was working on required a bit of concentration and lots of precision. He liked this kind of work, and he was used to it. Some days the rhythm of the work kept him moving at a good pace and the day would pass quickly. He was good at what he did. Always had been. He was good with his hands and good with people. Especially kids. Although Telly didn't have any kids yet, some day ... when the right woman came along. But there was plenty of time for that. He was only 27. Tall and slim, he walked with his back straight, almost like a plank. His thick sandy brown hair framed a face already rugged with the vestiges of the outdoors and years of work, honest backbreaking work. On the weekends it was construction, building, yard-work, anything he could get his hands on. Telly loved working outdoors. On a hot day, he often took his shirt off to get a nice tan on his arms and torso. Telly enjoyed the work. It paid the bills and the extra money he picked up now and then went to his savings, for his dream house. Ever since he saw a picture of a tiny house, he had his heart set on one. He wanted to design and build his own tiny house on wheels. And if he did it himself he could save money, but it would take a while ... hey who's counting? Telly smiled to himself as he thought about his tiny house, letting the rhythm of his job take over, mingling with the buzz of his sander as he kept it moving in the direction of the wood grain, smoothing the wood, making sure it didn't leave any swirl marks. The day went quickly and soon it was time to pick up the kids.

Telly got into in his reliable old pickup, dropped it at the bus depot, picked up the school bus, and drove a short distance along a well-travelled road he knew so well. It was a familiar routine, like clockwork, where he went every afternoon during the week. He didn't have to wait too long. Promptly at 2:30 p.m. the door opened and the kids rushed out, all at once, talking and laughing. Telly watched as his kids climbed on the bus. He had a good route, a long route that went a few miles out of town. He didn't mind, actually he liked the fact that he had this route. It took him farther out in the countryside, outside of town, and he enjoyed the scenery along the way. It didn't take long to get out of town. Rocky Flats was a small town with a Main Street and stores along both sides of it. Not much more to it than that, but you had most everything you needed.

The kids on Telly's route lived in the countryside. Bryan was the first to get off. He lived with his Dad, a single parent, in a brown house on the right side of the road. He was a cool kid. He liked to be by himself. A little bit of a nerd, you might say, but a good kid nevertheless.

"Hey, Bryan, have a good weekend. See you Monday!"

"Oh yeah, see you," Bryan shouted as he got off the bus.

Telly drove down the road to Annie's house. Annie's Dad was still at work, but Annie's Mom was by the side of the road, as she usually was when he picked Annie up and dropped her off. He knew Annie was a bit embarrassed by her Mom sometimes, but she didn't say that, really. Telly could tell Annie loved her Mom and knew that her Mom loved her too. Telly watched as Annie's Mom gave her a hug and took her lunch bag as they started to walk back to the house. "Bye, Telly," Annie said as she turned to wave. Telly waved back.

Next to leave was Liz. She was ready to go. As always, the minute he opened the door she bounced out, and made a beeline for her house. He barely got the words out, "Bye, Liz, see you Monday," before she disappeared across the yard into her house. Telly watched her to be sure she made it home safely. He knew from talking to Liz that she was a latchkey kid as her parents were still at work.

Just a couple more stops. Ron got up as Telly approached his house. Ron had just had a growth spurt. He was already taller and bigger than the other kids. Ron had a good, easy-going personality and was laid back. He sauntered to the front of the bus and nodded to Telly as his stop came. Telly nodded back, as Ron jumped off the last step and went inside a house with a fence around it, where he lived with his parents and his little sister Darla. Ron had mentioned that although she was only 4-years-old, Darla was already excited about riding the yellow school bus and could hardly wait.

The last stop was Billy's house, a small wood-framed cottage. Billy was wiry and thin, smaller than the other kids. He was smart. But he was not a show-off or stuck-up at all. He lived with his Mom, a single parent. Billy got off the bus and said "Bye, Telly!"

"See you Monday, Billy!"

Telly was done for the day. It was Friday. He was ready for some downtime and a bit of relaxation. It had been a long day since he got up at 6 a.m. After dropping the bus off, he got in his truck and stopped to get a beer at the watering hole. He saw a few folks who had gotten off work already. It's a good place to hang out, he thought as he sat on the barstool. Ray came up and pulled up a stool "Hey, Telly, heard you were looking for another Saturday gig."

"Hi, Ray, you got something for me?"

"Buddy, we could use another pair of hands tomorrow. I'm getting a crew together to install new asphalt roof shingles on old man Caper's house."

"Count me in. What time do you want me there?"

"Six in the morning ... we'll get started early and keep going until we're done. Bring your lunch."

Telly smiled. He was pleased to get another day of work outdoors doing what he liked, as he thought about the rhythm of the work and the hammers pounding the nails in. He was concerned about being outdoors as he was already tanned, so sometimes he had to watch it. If he were out too long, he might get a nasty sunburn. He took a swig of beer. That tasted so good going down. After finishing his beer, he got up and paid. Tomorrow was Saturday, and he had to grab a few supplies to get ready for the day.

Chapter 3

SATURDAY, 2 DAYS EARLIER

Telly woke up at 5 a.m. on Saturday, his alarm blaring with radio station chattering. He yawned and stretched his feet over the frame at the end of the bed. It felt great to start the day early. Telly pulled some clean clothes from the laundry basket, since he hadn't had the time to fold and put them away. He pulled on an old T-shirt, a pair of faded jeans, and white work socks. He rummaged in his closet to find the right pair of shoes, the kind that kept him from slipping. He found an old pair of tennis shoes he used for roofing jobs, and he put those on. He also found a large chunk of foam he could sit on while working on the roof, to give him some extra traction and to keep the heat from the asphalt shingles from burning his butt.

Telly made his way to his small kitchen and started the coffee. *Man,* he thought. *There is nothing like a good cup of coffee, dark-roasted and black, just the way he likes it.* He scrambled four eggs in the frying pan and threw in four slabs of bacon at the same time. The kitchen was cozy, with barely enough room for a small table and a couple of chairs. Telly sat down in one of the chairs and ate his breakfast while it was hot. He poured the rest of the coffee in a large travel mug to take with him. He quickly sliced a couple of huge red juicy tomatoes, got some bread out, and slapped them together to make a couple of tomato sandwiches. He pulled on his tool belt, then got into his reliable old blue pickup. It was only 5:40 a.m. He had plenty of time to get there and get situated. A beautiful day; you needed that for a roofing job.

By 6, he met up with Ray and the crew at old man Caper's house. The house was small, and the old man lived alone. The shingle roof had been patched over the years, and it badly needed to be replaced. They quickly got started, taking down the gutters first, then nailing huge sheets of blue tarp over the edge of the house, letting it hang over the side and on top of the lawn. They threw some boards on it to secure the tarp at the ends where it lay flat in the yard. Telly used a flat-head shovel to remove the old shingles and easily popped the rusty nails right off along with the old felt. The blue tarp was a time saver. All he had to do was to toss those old shingles and the old felt over the roof, and they'd fall on the blue tarp and slide down to the ground. Whatever was on the blue tarp would end up in the dumpster.

Roofing was hard and dangerous work. Some guys don't take roofing jobs because of that. A couple of years ago there was an accident, and a guy got hurt real bad. Most of the crew didn't have health insurance, so when they got hurt, each man did what he could to get it taken care of depending on what he could afford to pay. Sometimes you just made do and tried to take care of it yourself. It's the way it goes on these jobs. Telly was not too fond of heights, but he knew that if he thought about it, it only got worse. So Telly tried not to think about it, not to look down, and just concentrated on his job, what he had to do. Soon he was installing new felt, settled into the rhythm of the job, and into the routine. *Bam ... bam ... bam!* The air was filled with the sound of slap tackers stapling the new felt.

The beauty of starting this early was to beat the sun for a few hours. They would work throughout the morning and take a late lunch. Nobody stopped unless you had to pee. Telly kept going, and soon it was time for lunch. He wasn't very hungry but was glad to take a break. Telly ate his tomato sandwiches by his truck where he had parked it in the shade. He wiped his lips with the back of his hand, as he savored the juicy taste with each bite of the thick tomato slices. He didn't want a heavy meal on a job like this. He took swigs from his coffee mug. He had kept it with him, like an extra tool. When he finished, Telly rested a bit in the shade and chatted with the other guys.

Ray was busy making sure they were on track and getting the job done. There was a bonus if they could get it done today. Ray had a good crew with mostly guys he'd worked with before, and they all knew each other. Roofing was not rocket science, but the quality of the work would show through. He didn't want to get called back in the middle of the night or any time when it was raining. Ray knew his job and had planned it out beforehand. There were a few problems he had to work through but no real hitches. He liked working on roofs. It's a specialty that he learned in his early days. This kind of roofing job didn't come too often, but the word had gotten around that he was steady, dependable, and did good work. Folks around here liked that and liked him.

Sometimes Ray tried out a new guy on a job to see how that went, and sometimes it worked out. It wasn't for everyone, though. He had been lucky so far. Actually, common sense had a lot to do with it. He checked people out a bit before he hired them. In a small town, you knew almost everyone. Every now and then someone new came to town, looking for work. Ray prided himself on being able to assess people, and to get a feel for them within a few minutes of having met and talked to them. Today, he had a new man on the crew. A guy had just arrived in town and was looking to make a few bucks. All cash, paid at the end of the day. Ray had talked to him the day before and got the sense he would do an honest day of work and be dependable. The guy's name was Steve. He was scrawny, and he looked like it had been a few days since he had a good shave. When Ray met Steve the day before he had given him an advance which would come out of his pay, so he could get a room and a hot bath. Steve seemed happy to be getting the roofing work today. Ray started him off on some grunt work, but Steve didn't seem to mind. He apparently had solid muscles under his shirt, and he was not a stranger to hard work. Ray looked around and was pleased with this crew today. He had a good crew. It had worked out well.

The work continued at a good clip after lunch. The job was going at such a good pace that the work would be done a bit earlier than expected. They were already putting down new shingles with nail guns. Around suppertime, they finished the job. Ray did a final inspection, and then told the crew to clean up. He got a couple of other guys to come in the evening to pick up all the trash and empty the tarps in the dumpster. It was a good day. Ray was feeling generous, and he told everyone to meet him at the Big Blue Moon Saloon, the favorite bar for working men in Rocky Flats. He was going to buy everyone a beer and give each of them their pay. The crew, including Telly, met there. After Telly got a beer, he sat down and chilled out. He enjoyed the cold beer, taking slow, deep sips.

Life was good. It had been a good week, and Telly had some extra money in his pocket. He had managed his savings well, had watched with satisfaction as it grew, taking him closer to his dream house. His pickup was already paid off. The roomy crew cab was a plus. He didn't mind the scratches and dents; they added character.

Telly got up to go. "Ray, I'm heading out."

"Appreciate your help today, man. Are you going to the cookout tomorrow at John Decker's place?"

"I'm thinking about it," Telly said.

"The whole crew's invited," Ray said. "My sister Jen will be there; she's back in town."

Telly gave him a surprised look. He hadn't seen Jen in years. He remembered seeing her when she was still in pigtails. Last he heard she had gone off to college.

"Okay, Ray, I'll see you at the cookout."

Chapter 4

SUNDAY, 1 DAY EARLIER

When Sunday rolled around, Telly slept late. He got up at 10, and he made coffee and breakfast. He skipped the eggs, as he had heard that too much cholesterol was bad. Telly was only 27, but he didn't want to overdo the egg thing. He needed his body to last as long as it could, and it was in his best interest to keep it in great shape. *Well, hell with the bacon too.* Telly thought. *I'll skip both and just whip up some batter and make pancakes. I've got a couple of ripe bananas I can mash and throw in the batter. I haven't had banana pancakes in a long time; that sounds good.*

Telly was used to being single. He had his place to himself, ate what he liked, and was a decent cook for the kinds of things he liked to eat. He managed just fine. Occasionally he went out on dates. His sister Sarah was always trying to fix him up with one of her girlfriends. She was only a couple of years older but thought nothing of bossing him around. Telly loved his older sister, but he could only stand to be around her for a short time. *A big sis is not the person a man needed to hover over him,* Telly thought. He picked up his cell phone to call Sarah, as they hadn't talked for awhile. Sarah was busy with her own life. She was married to Dave and had two adorable kids, ages 2 and 3. A little too young; in Telly's mind, they were not little people until they were 4. But he loved them anyway. Sarah picked up the phone on the third ring. She sounded harried. "He ... hello...."

"Hey, how's my big sis?"

"Telly, how's my little brother? I haven't heard from you in ages. Have you been busy?"

Telly laughed. "I have been working my butt off. You doing OK?"

"You know me. I've got my hands full with the kids." Sarah sighed. "Some days I don't know how I do it."

"Say hi to the kids and hub for me."

"Hey, don't be a stranger. Come by for Sunday dinner tonight."

"I'm going to a cook-out, hang out with the guys. Give me a raincheck?"

"OK, but I'm going to hold you to the next one. Be here next Sunday."

"Yup, see ya then. Bye."

Telly had a couple of hours to kill before the cookout. Time to throw in the wash and grab a six-pack for his contribution.

Telly got to the cookout in good time. They were just getting started. No big deal; this was Sunday afternoon, and everybody was relaxed and taking their time. The guys didn't care what was on the menu as long as you could throw it on the grill and eat it. Telly knew most of the guys; there were a couple he didn't know but had seen around town. He nodded to them. It was a friendly group. There would be time to talk and get around. Telly picked up a beer and popped the cap. It tasted good. He really should cut down on the beers someday, but right now that was the last thing on his mind.

Ray came up. "Hey, man."

Telly smiled. He really liked Ray.

"I'm glad you made it," said Ray. He tilted this head to the guy standing next to him. "You know John…" Telly nodded.

"Hey, thanks for coming. Make yourself at home. Enjoy the party," John said in a booming voice as they shook hands.

John was the big cheese in town. Every now and then he would throw a cookout or party. A lot of guys had worked for him over the years, and he liked to get to know his guys on the job and off the job. In a small town, it was easy to do that. Although John had the jobs, he left the hiring to the foremen and leads. That way he didn't have to handle everything. John liked to show off his home, which was larger than any of the other homes in town and, being a businessman, he wrote off a lot of these gatherings as business expenses. John could cozy up to politicians and smooch babies just as easily. Whatever the reason for coming, most guys enjoyed an afternoon off to shoot the breeze and hang out.

Telly surveyed the crowd and was surprised to see the new guy Steve there. Ray had quickly introduced him yesterday, but he didn't get a chance to talk to him. He knew Steve was a good worker, and a good person to have on his team. He walked over to Steve, who looked a little out of place, as he hardly knew anyone.

"Hey man, how's it going? I'm Telly. I saw you working at old man Capers house yesterday."

"I'm Steve. Yea, I saw you on the roof yesterday..."

"You new in town?"

"Just got in Friday. Got lucky with the roofing job."

"Yep, that was a good gig. I do that every now and then," Telly said. He grinned. "You planning on staying awhile?"

"Got no plans yet. Just hanging out for now. Nice town."

"Glad to meet you. It looks like the burgers are ready. Wanna grab a bite?"

"Sure, I'm starved."

They got plates and grabbed a couple of burgers each. Telly piled on onions, pickles, and tomatoes before he bit into his burger. It was medium and juicy, just the way he liked it.

"Iced tea?" Telly looked up to see a petite brunette carrying icy glasses of tea on a tray. She flashed him a friendly smile.

"Sure, iced tea sounds good. I'll have some. I'm Telly."

"Hi, I'm Jen. Ray's younger sister."

Telly smiled. "You sure have grown up. So you've been away to college?"

"Yes. I'm going to the state college. I've got one more year to go, then I'm done."

"So what are you studying?"

"Environmental studies."

Telly gave a long whistle. "You must really like school."

"Always did. Don't get me wrong. I love this town, but I also wanted to do more … and learn..."

"I left town for a while too, after high school. I tried the community college for a semester, then I decided it wasn't for me. Now I drive a school bus, work at the cabinet shop, and do construction, roofing, and other jobs around here. I never was that much into schooling."

Jen handed Telly his iced tea. "Here's your tea. I gotta go. I'll see you around."

"Yep, see you around." Telly watched her go, admiring the way she balanced her tray easily as she moved. *She's got some waitressing experience*, he thought. Telly figured that she was about 20 or 21, maybe six or seven years younger. *She's definitely grown up*, he thought. *Not the way I remember her, a little girl in pigtails.*

The party was starting to wind down as people drifted off and left. Telly got up. On the way out, he saw Steve. "Hey, buddy, can I give you a lift?"

"Sure, I was going to walk, but I'll take a lift."

Telly gave Steve a ride back into town. Steve lived in a rooming house that looked a bit run down, at the edge of town, across from the elementary school. It was a large house that had been chopped up into rooms that were rented out. The rooms were rented to single men or women, although it was mostly men. The rooms were basic, no frills, a place to put your head down at night, lay on a bed. Down the hallway, you cleaned up with a hot shower. Not much more that a man like Steve needed at this time. Sometimes Dottie, who owned and ran the place, would cook a meal, a nice home-cooked meal, to give the boarders a real treat. It wasn't fancy, but it just felt more like home to have a hot meal sometimes. Dottie was getting on in years, and it wasn't something she could do every night. And really, it was more special when it was done only every so often.

Tonight was one of those nights. Dottie had taped a note on the door "Hot meal tonight at 6 p.m." Steve turned to Telly and said, "Would you like to come to dinner?" Telly didn't have anything planned for the evening, having blown off his sister. So he thought, *why not*?

"Sure, thanks. I'll stay for dinner."

They were a bit early, so Steve offered to give him a tour of the place and a walk outside in the yard. The first floor had an entryway and a central hall. The living room and dining room were on either side, the kitchen was in the back, and there was a hall bathroom. Upstairs were the rented rooms. Steve's room was small but comfortable. He had a single bed, a chest of drawers, and a bedside table with a lamp on it. The full bathroom with a shower and tub was next to the room at the end of the hallway, and it was shared with the other guests on the floor. Dottie had another floor above and each floor had its own bathroom.

They went back to the dining room where half a dozen people had gathered already. The food was laid on a table, buffet style. There was bread, a salad, a bowl of mashed potatoes, a plate of green beans, a dish of carrots, and two other baked dishes that were casseroles. Steve led the way, and they each grabbed a plate. It was all vegetables, home cooked, and it sure smelled good. Telly was surprised at how much he liked the meal, and somewhat relieved it didn't come with meat, as he'd had enough of burgers at the cookout.

It turned out that Dottie was the entertainment as well as the cook. After dinner, she regaled everyone with stories ... oh she had so many stories to tell. Dottie had grown up in Rocky Flats and knew everyone. Her folks had owned this house, and it was passed down to her. She loved to cook and talk so it was natural that she assumed this role and took over the rooming house, although she preferred to call herself the innkeeper. Dottie had a photographic memory; she remembered folks that passed through and told fascinating stories about them. Telly found himself drawn into the stories. He thoroughly enjoyed hearing Dottie talk. He could tell some of the other people had come for the meal but quickly ended up staying and having a good time afterwards. When it was over, he reluctantly turned to go.

Telly drove home, took a shower, and called it a night. It had been a great day, but he was ready for bed. Tomorrow was Monday, the start of another week.

Chapter 5

MONDAY

He heard a muffled sneeze. Telly quickly opened the door of the nearest classroom, but he didn't see anyone. He waited. More muffled sounds ... from the direction of a cabinet. Telly dashed across the room, yanked opened the cabinet door, and saw Billy, all cramped up inside. He was small enough that he could curl up and fit inside. Billy blinked his eyes in the light, then slowly registered relief when he realized that it was Telly.

"Billy, are you OK? What happened ... why are you hiding in a cabinet?"

Billy's voice was shaking. "I ... I didn't want to go."

"Is anyone else here?" Telly spoke gently, yet urgently.

"I don't know ... if someone else but ... I didn't hear anything and ... I don't know," Billy stammered. Telly gently pulled his right arm and shoulder, slowly eased him out of the cabinet, and carried him out. He stood him up and held on to Billy as he tried to stand up by himself, stomping his legs to get the cramps out of them.

"Here, hold on to me and stretch your legs one at a time," Telly said.

"I'm still a bit wobbly, but I'm going to take a few steps and stand on my own."

"That's good, Billy. Easy does it."

"Thanks." Billy was determined to stand up on his own and walk, and he did it.

"C'mon Billy, let's go out and look. Maybe someone else is here."

"No, wait," Billy said. "Let's go to the principal's office and talk on the intercom. If anyone is here, they'll be able to hear us." One teacher, the one who had been there the longest, also did double duty as the principal - on a part-time basis. Actually, she spent more time teaching in the classroom than in her office.

They headed to her office. Telly turned on the intercom. "This is Telly."

"And Billy. We're trying to find out what happened. Is anyone else here? If you're here, please go to the principal's office. Immediately."

Telly and Billy waited and waited. Telly repeated the message over the intercom a couple more times. Nobody came. Telly scrolled through the numbers on his cell phone and called. Starting with Billy's Mom. She answered on the second ring. "Hello."

"Hi, this is Telly the bus driver. I have Billy with me."

"What … where are you? What's going on?"

"We're at the school. Billy is fine. We have a situation."

"I want to speak to Billy," his Mom said.

"Here he is," Telly said as he handed the phone over to Billy.

"Hi, Mom, I'm all right ... just a little scared."

"Billy, tell me what happened!"

"Mom, I don't know what happened but everyone else is gone. Telly and I are still at the school. I don't know where everyone went. Have you heard anything?"

"No, but I'm going to call around and check. I want you to call me as soon as you find out anything, OK? Tell Telly to bring you home as soon as he can. I love you."

"Ok Mom. Love you too. Bye." Billy turned to Telly. "She's going to let us know if she hears anything."

Telly made a few more calls of his own. He contacted the sheriff's office first, then John Decker and Ray Rogers and told them what had happened. Immediately, they were on their way. By this time, the phone had started ringing with calls from worried parents who didn't know where their kids were. They should have been home by now. Telly left a voice mail message on the school phone with reassurances that the sheriff and help were on the way.

He looked up as the principal's office door opened, and a few people who he recognized as parents walked in. Telly quickly brought them up to date on what had happened. They sprang into action. They picked up the phone to answer calls. Soon the principal's office and the connecting front reception area were filled with people working the phones and getting the word out.

Telly and Billy decided to check outside again. They walked around the backyard and the play ground areas but didn't see or hear anything suspicious. Then they walked around to the front. As they turned to leave, Telly noticed large tire tracks on the driveway going toward the road. He didn't recognize them, but he could clearly see that large vehicles had made the tracks. He looked to see where they were going. The tracks led to the road and turned right, heading out of town. Telly jumped in his school bus and said to Billy, "Hop in."

Billy was all too glad to get out of there.

Chapter 6

After dropping off the school bus, Telly and Billy switched vehicles and got into Telly's truck. He drove slowly, keeping an eye out for any signs of the missing children and teachers. He didn't know where he was going; he just kept going out of town. Telly drove three, five ... then a few more miles.

Still there was no sign of them. He glanced over at Billy to see how he was doing. Billy seemed to have gotten over his shakiness and was a bit calmer. So Telly attempted to talk to him, gently, to find out what had happened. "Billy, can you tell me what you remember ... can you think back, to what happened?"

Billy collected his thoughts and closed his eyes for a moment. "I heard loud noises and some shouting. I couldn't see anyone, but the teacher told us to remain calm and to stay in our room." He wrinkled his forehead and then continued. "I tried to look out the window, but it was too far away from me and ... I couldn't see anything. All of a sudden the door opened

... and ... everyone screamed and panicked." Billy's voice shook slightly. "In the confusion, I crawled inside one of the cabinets and hid there. I stayed there and lost all track of time. I didn't move until you opened the door, and I saw ... you." Billy sighed.

"I had almost given up and was on my way out when I heard a sneeze," Telly said. "Imagine my surprise when I opened the door and saw you. I'm just so glad you're safe." Telly looked over his right shoulder and gave Billy a warm smile.

Telly called his sister on his cell. Otherwise, he knew she would be worrying about him. "Hi, sis, I want to tell you ..."

"Oh my God," she interrupted. "I just heard on the radio. I know something is very wrong ... can you tell me anything? Nobody knows what's going on."

"Sarah, I'm with Billy. And we're trying to find out what happened. We're in my pickup and checking things out. I'll call you later when we know something. We're fine."

Sarah sounded worried, "Well I don't know anything but call me as soon as you find out."

While Telly was driving and talking to his sister, Billy had been looking out his side of the window. He caught a glimpse of something glinting on the side of the road, and immediately grabbed Telly's arm and shouted. "Stop! Now! I see something!"

Telly quickly ended his call to Sarah, "I need to check something out now. Got to go!" He stomped on the brakes and stopped the truck. "Billy where is it?"

Billy turned around in his seat and pointed back at a spot on the right side of the road, where they had just passed. "There ... something bright and shining ... see it?"

Telly slowly backed up about 50 feet. He saw sunlight reflecting off something metal. Telly and Billy jumped out of the truck to take a closer look. It was a metal watchband sticking out of the ground. Telly gave Billy a squeeze on his shoulder, "Good catch, Billy! You sure got sharp eyes. I totally missed it."

Telly carefully looked around for anything else out of the ordinary. He saw tracks of shoe prints near where the watch was. The tracks were headed northeast, away from the road. Telly and Billy followed the shoe prints, being careful not to step on them. There were quite a few sets of different shoes; most were small, a few were larger. It was hard to say how many there were. As they followed the shoe prints to see where they were headed, it became clear the people weren't running or jogging; they were just walking. The shoe prints were all headed in the same direction. Telly was not a tracker by any means, but he had plenty of common sense. He was getting ready to check his map when they came upon a large clearing surrounded by huge rock piles. It stood out from the rest of the area. The tracks went inside the clearing and stopped there.

He called Billy's Mom with the news. She picked up on the first ring, "Hey, this is Telly, here with Billy."

"I'm so glad you called. How's the search? How's Billy? Have you found anything?"

Telly exclaimed, "Billy saw it – someone's watch!"

"What! Oh my gosh..."

"Billy's a smart kid. I drove right past it, but he stopped me ... so we went back to check it out. It turned out to be a watch sticking out from the ground. We saw shoe prints and followed them to this clearing encircled by huge rock piles."

Billy reached out his hand and snatched the phone. "Hi, Mom."

"Billy, I'm so proud of you! I know you wanted to help."

"Hey, Mom, can I stay with Telly some more?"

"I..."

"*Please* Mom ... *I want to!*"

"Well ... just be careful. Keep in touch and call me soon."

"OK, bye Mom."

Telly and Billy circled carefully around the outside perimeter of the area but didn't see anyone behind the rocks. It appeared to be a dead end. Telly was stumped.

Chapter 7

The scene back at the school was one of pandemonium, as parents and community volunteers descended, eager to help and get started. Search parties were forming and soon on their way out of town. People were prepared to search through the night, if they had to. It was like a circus atmosphere with activity, noise, and throngs of people moving and hurrying as fast as they could, as if that would take them one step closer to finding the children.

A reporter from the radio was on the air talking about the search groups being organized for an all-night effort. "This is Ami Adams reporting from WEXE. I have with me Ray Rogers, who is coordinating this search effort." Turning to him, she said, "Ray, can you tell us about the search?"

"We've formed search parties and organized shifts. Our first shift has already left. They branched out from the school. We will have shifts revolving through the night. Search parties will be going out 24/7," Ray said.

He added, "Thanks to everyone who has volunteered. If you are interested, please call or come to the school to sign up for a shift. We need you."

"Thank you Ray, we'll be back with you for updates." She paused. "Now, behind us, tables and tents have been set up. There are several stations." Ami viewed the scene and turned to John. "John Decker, I understand you are spearheading this effort. What do we have here?" she asked.

"We have set up a phone/communications station, a volunteer station, a first-aid station, a supply station, and a food and drink station. Other stations will be set up as needed, but we started with the basics first."

The reporter tilted the mike closer to John. "So if someone wants to call us with information or to volunteer do you have a toll free number?"

"Yes, please call 1-888-KID-FIND."

Ami repeated the number, "Please call 1-888-KID-FIND if you have any information or if you would like to volunteer." She was going to be there all night. She looked over to where the parents were anxiously waiting, as a tent was quickly being set up for them with a radio, phone line, chairs, tables, and a few cots. Updates were going to be offered throughout the night.

There was excitement and heightened expectations as the search groups left, one by one. Those who remained behind were busy manning the 1-888 phone line, carrying more supplies in, and signing up more people who had come to volunteer. Ray had already left with a search party. His sister Jen was at the food and drink station setting up drinks and cooking some hot dogs. Dottie had rounded up some of the rooming house residents, and she was taking charge of the volunteer tent. She had her hands full coordinating the volunteer sign-ups. All in all, the stations dealt with the emergency of the situation as best as they could. People focused on the work and kept busy, determined to block out any thoughts about the possibility that something worse could have happened.

Chapter 8

Telly and Billy searched the clearing and then went farther out to look beyond the rocks. He glanced at Billy, who looked tired and hungry. "How are you holding up?"

Billy shrugged. He kept up the pace and kept on walking. He didn't complain, not even once.

Telly remembered that he had some candy bars in the glove compartment of his truck. He gestured to Billy, and they walked back. Telly grabbed a couple of bars and offered them to Billy.

Billy was all too eager to eat the candy bars. He quickly grasped one and ripped off the wrapper, mumbling "Umm ... umm" as he stuffed it in his mouth.

It was now nearing dusk. Telly motioned to Billy to get in the truck. Telly turned the headlights on and took out the flashlights from his glove box. He sure was glad he had stuck them in there. Farther from the clearing he could see mountains, way up ahead. Telly and Billy drove down the road. Night was settling over the area accompanied by the chirping of insects. It was a clear night.

Billy was quiet, and he didn't say anything for a while. But suddenly, he turned to Telly. "Will we ever find them? Will we ever see Bryan, Ron, Annie, Liz and the others?" Telly had told him about the search parties and what was happening back at the school. Billy had a worried look on his face. He was eager to find them, but the excitement of finding the watch and the anticipation of finding the children had diminished with each passing hour. He wanted them to be found. He wanted to, so badly, but his heart sank with the sunset. It just didn't make sense how all these people could have disappeared ... vanished ... poof, into thin air.

Telly was starting to worry, but he kept the worries to himself and didn't share them with Billy. "We'll find them. We have search parties and people all over town who are out looking." Billy didn't respond. He seemed lost in his own thoughts. Telly hoped Billy would be reassured by knowing everyone was doing what they could.

As he looked out in the dark, Telly fought a rising feeling of despair. He thought, *Is there a God? How can God let it happen? God help us all.*

Telly felt at a loss as to what he could do next. He checked his gas gauge. It was getting low. He checked his map. The next town, Big Bear, was about seven miles away, so he headed there. He pulled into the gas station at the edge of town.

Finding some stale coffee left in his mug, Telly downed the last drop as he sat in the truck with Billy.

He called Billy's Mom, gave her an update, and assured her that Billy was all right.

She told him what was happening back at the school. "It could be a while before the search party makes its way there."

"Well then, Billy and I are going to stay here and look around some more. We still have some light, and I've brought my flashlights."

"But I want to see Billy home soon ... it's getting late!" The worry in her voice came through loud and clear.

Billy grabbed the phone before Telly could say anything, "Hi Mom!"

"Billy, are you all right?"

"Yes, Mom. I don't want you to worry. I'll be fine here with Telly."

"I thought you'd be back tonight already. Telly should bring you home *now*."

"I'm not ready to come back yet. I'll be all right."

"You're *sure* you want to do this?"

"I *have* to do this. I want to stay with Telly tonight."

"I need some time to think about this. Have Telly call me in a little while, OK?"

"Sure Mom."

"Be careful. I love you, kid."

"Love you too, Mom. Bye."

Chapter 9

By now it was dark. Trained search dogs and their handlers had arrived as volunteers to help search for the missing people. They immediately went into action. The reporter interviewed several people who were allegedly experts, as if they were the authorities and could give the answers. Of course, no one knew, and no one gave the same answer. Everyone had different theories as to what they thought had happened. They also didn't have any great ideas on how to find the children, beyond what had already been put into motion. It was apparent that people were still in shock after hearing the news, as if to say "Did I really hear that?" "What happened?" "How could they have vanished into thin air?" There were more questions than answers, and nobody was an expert, as nothing like this had ever happened in the town. No one really knew what happened.

More and more people had gathered in the school area. The sheriff had blocked off certain areas, and a few people wearing orange vests with light-reflecting strips were directing traffic and people. The first parking lot was full, so a designated area had been set aside for more cars, trucks, and vehicles. It was becoming better organized. A station had been set up to interview the townspeople to see if they had seen or heard anything. Nothing, no matter how small, was going to be overlooked. The reporter was giving out the hot-line number from time to time. She was telling people to call if they have any information at all. They would record any information, big or small. A few people were set up to help track down the leads. Parents and relatives of the missing were given a separate private hot line for the families only. By now a list of everyone who went missing had been generated and verified. Family members could call their private hot line number to find out about their loved ones, 24/7.

Chapter 10

The old man was sitting at the counter in the gas station. Telly went inside to pay. As he walked towards the dingy little one-room gas station, Telly could hear the radio, blasting away. The reporter was talking about the search parties and repeated the 1-888-KID-FIND number.

Telly asked the old man if he had any information. The old man shook his head in disbelief, "Out in these parts of the country it's quiet. Folks go about their business. We don't have a lot of crime."

"Have you noticed or seen anything odd in these parts lately?"

"Nothing like this, in all the years I've been here." He shook his head for emphasis.

Telly thanked him, walked out, pumped his gas, and got back in the truck. He didn't start the engine right away. He wanted time to think. Although Rocky Flats was about 27 miles away, Telly thought it was odd that the shoe prints had disappeared a few miles from here. The old man in the gas station had not seen anything unusual. *He's an old man,* Telly thought. *His hearing wasn't that sharp, maybe he couldn't see that well either.*

Since they were already here, Telly decided to take a look around this town and see what he could find. Big Bear was much smaller than Rocky Flats. The Main Street was a couple hundred yards long and consisted of only a few stores other than the gas station. Here in these parts of the country there were no fast-food joints. The only restaurant in town had closed by now, as had all the stores, except for the general store. Telly and Billy went in to stock up their supplies and get something to eat and drink. He grabbed a couple of blankets, bottles of water and soda, and looked around for some food. There were some sandwiches, home-made apple pies, and a small selection of snack items. He looked at Billy and nodded for him to go ahead and pick out what he wanted.

The cashier didn't know much about what had happened. Her shift had started at 3:00 p.m., and she had been working. When Telly told her about the missing children at the school in Rocky Flats, she listened intently to every word he said. "I haven't seen any strangers come in today. It's been a slow day. Have you checked with the old man in the gas station?" she suggested.

"Yep, talked to him on the way in town. He hadn't seen anything either."

She finished checking him out. "Well good luck. Hope you find them soon."

Telly nodded his thanks, picked up his purchases, and left with Billy.

Chapter 11

After they put the supplies in the truck, Telly called Billy's Mom again. "Mind if I keep Billy with me tonight?" He kept his voice calm and reassuring. "We have blankets and plenty of food and water. We'll be fine. It doesn't get that cold out here at this time of the year."

She hesitated. "I don't like the thought of Billy out there when he should be here, at home, with me."

"It's been quiet out here. We haven't seen signs of anyone yet."

"Billy should have been back by now."

"You know how much Billy wants to help. This means a lot to him."

She thought about what Billy had said, what he wanted to do, and how much this meant to him.

"I promise I'll take good care of him," Telly said reassuringly.

"I know you will…"

"Billy is determined to be part of this, and he's *not* ready to go home yet."

She knew that time was valuable and that every minute in the search could get them a step closer to finding the children. Finally she said, "Fine, keep Billy with you and make sure he gets enough food and sleep. Call me in the morning."

"Will do. You get some sleep too."

It was time to head back to the clearing. Telly wanted to check it out again. They ate quickly then sat on a rock next to the clearing and looked up at the sky. It was a beautiful night with the stars and the moon peeking out boldly. He wished that he had a telescope, as if it would bring him closer to the answer ... and to a higher being.

Darkness enveloped them. Telly glanced at Billy, and he could tell the boy was getting drowsy. Telly proceeded to carry a now very sleepy Billy back to the truck, where he had cleared the back seat to make a comfortable place for Billy. He carefully laid Billy down, then covered him with the blanket and tucked him in for the night. He watched Billy as he lay there sleeping, so small and thin. He wasn't a praying man, but tonight he almost wished he was.

Chapter 12

T he first search party had come back to the school empty-handed. Most of the people were going to get some rest and head back out again early in the morning. Although the second search party had not yet returned, another search party had been formed with the dogs and left. Another dispatch was scheduled to go out at daybreak to the area where Telly had last seen the shoe prints.

The interviews were moving along at a good clip, but no helpful information had turned up yet. By all accounts, it had seemed a fairly normal day with everyone going about their business. Nobody had seen or heard anything out of the ordinary. It would be a good while before they could finish talking to everyone and follow up with all the leads.

The reporter was giving another update. This time you could hear how tired she was. Still, she put on a cheery smile and continued to talk about the search-party shifts that were scheduled into the night and the next day. Everyone wanted to help. No one's efforts were refused. She scanned the area while she described to the listeners what was happening. Bright lights had been set up and the tents were lit. It looked like a carnival scene. The phone lines were buzzing with people calling in. This was attracting so-called experts and weirdos out of the woodwork. There was no shortage of people who wanted to give their opinions as to what had happened. No caller was turned away. Everyone was interviewed as if what each had to say was equally important. The town was running on adrenaline, and time was running out.

Chapter 13

TUESDAY

By dawn, it was a new day fresh with promises and faith aplenty. The shifts had rotated throughout the night and into the day. The day shift started early, before the break of dawn. Few people went home. They took naps or slept in their cars, trucks, vans, or on makeshift cots in the tents. The morning news came on at 5 a.m. with Ami Adams reporting. Turning the mike to John, she said, "John, I understand this is a very organized effort, to your credit, and to the many volunteers who have worked throughout the night. Are you expecting to have more help today?"

"We've received many calls from people who are volunteering. I've talked to some experts. I'm expecting them to arrive today with equipment and sensors and to hopefully provide clues as to what may have happened."

"John, thank you. We will be talking to you again later today."

Ami interviewed Ray about new leads and a heads-up on what was being planned for the day. Ami wanted Ray to provide quick updates on the search parties. "Ray can you tell us about the search parties?"

"Search parties have been going throughout the night. We've added search dogs. The night shift has rotated off, and the dawn shift left before daybreak. We also sent a dispatch out to where we're tracking the shoe prints. We're doing all that we can."

"So they are getting close?"

"We've covered a lot of ground since yesterday afternoon. I expect we'll have some new information today."

"Thanks. We'll certainly look forward to that."

Chapter 14

Telly had not slept well. He woke up at the crack of dawn and tried to clear his thoughts. Usually something that had been bothering him would work its way up when he was sleeping, or he'd wake up from his dreams. But it didn't happen this time. His legs were cramped. He'd slept on the front seat of his truck, and his neck hurt. He yawned, stretched, and looked around. Billy was still sleeping, sprawled out on the back seat under the warm plaid blanket. Telly didn't want to wake him up yet. He decided he'd let him sleep a little longer while he found a place to get some hot breakfast. The closest place was Big Bear, where he remembered seeing a restaurant last night that was closed. He drove back there; fortunately, the restaurant was open.

Telly gently woke up Billy, and they walked in the restaurant. Inside, the smells of food cooking, sounds of sizzling on the grill, and the clinking of dishes greeted them. A handwritten sign on a board by the door –said, "Sit yourself. Any table." Spotting a table in a corner, they pulled out chairs and sat down. Telly realized how hungry he was. They eagerly studied the menu. As soon as the waitress came, he ordered for both. It would be a long day and Telly wanted to be sure they were well fueled. Soon the food was on the table and they dug in. It was delicious, and the coffee never tasted better. As he slowly sipped the warm coffee and food filled his belly, Telly began to feel this day would bring them answers. He called his boss at the cabinet shop, updated him quickly, and asked for the rest of the week off. Fortunately, Telly had an understanding boss who supported the search efforts. He had let Ray and the other workers leave early yesterday to help and told them they could take as much time off as they needed this week.

He looked up as the waitress, a pleasant looking older woman, came by and re-filled his coffee mug. "Hey, thanks," Telly said. "You heard about the disappearance at the school in Rocky Flats?"

"Honey, I've had my ears glued to the radio all night. It just tears me up. I can't believe what happened to the kids and the teachers."

Telly told her what he knew. "A search party will be coming this way after daybreak." He added cheerfully, "Hopefully they'll find something this time by bringing search dogs with them."

The waitress nodded as if she knew that it was the most natural thing, and they would absolutely, for sure, find them.

Telly asked her what she thought, and she suggested that he talk to the old man at the gas station. He smiled.

"I've already talked to him, but I'll stop by again on my way out of town."

They finished their breakfast and went on their way. Telly stopped at the gas station to find the old man, who remembered them from the previous night. Telly updated him and mentioned that a search party would be coming their way soon. The old man seemed to expect that, as he didn't seem too excited about it. Telly wanted to seek his counsel. "Do you have any suggestions?"

The old man said, "Just keep your eyes and ears open. Anything could happen out there."

"Thanks. I'll do that."

Telly drove out of the town thinking about the old man at the gas station. He didn't know how old he was, but it seemed the townspeople thought highly of him. He turned to Billy. "Billy, do you have any bright ideas?"

Billy thought for a moment and said, "I want to check out the shoe prints again." Telly drove back to the clearing and got out of the truck with Billy following closely. At the clearing, there were a lot of shoe prints. On closer look, Telly noticed that they came from the same direction into the clearing. They were dense and congregated inside the clearing but facing another direction, as if they were all looking at something or something had caught their attention. It was hard to tell how many, there were a lot of shoe prints for sure. Telly tried to count them but it was impossible. He took a few steps back and looked in the direction of the shoe prints, and then looked around to see if he could see what they might have been looking at.

The sky was clear blue with a few puffy clouds. There were no signs of the people whose footprints were left in the clearing. There was nothing more that they could see.

Telly had an idea to check out the direction they were facing from where they were standing. He took out a map, found where they were, then traced in that direction with his fingertip. His finger stopped at a town, a town called Blue. Telly decided he would head there with Billy. They got into the truck, and he started driving. Blue was 35 miles away. They got there in less than an hour. It was bigger than the last town but not much bigger. He could tell it was a newer town, as some of the buildings didn't have the run-down look. It looked like a normal town, with people going about their business. He pulled into the gas station and saw a man inside. Telly got out to talk to him, "Hey, I'm new to these parts. It looks like quite a new town you've got here."

The man looked at him and nodded.

"Heard about the disappearance of the school kids and the teachers in Rocky Flats?"

"Yep, it's all over the news." He shook his head, "Man, that's too bad."

"Have you heard or seen anything here?

"Nope."

"If you do, would you call this number?" Telly gave him the 888 number he'd written on a piece of torn paper.

"Yep."

Telly wanted to check out Blue, so he drove around slowly through town with Billy. By now it was mid-morning, and everything seemed normal. Yet something didn't quite feel right, and Telly couldn't put his finger on it. That feeling was nagging him, and he couldn't shake it off. He knew that, given time, it would percolate through and come to the surface. It was not time yet. It didn't take long for Telly to drive through the small town. Before he headed out, Telly pulled off to call Billy's Mom again. This time Billy grabbed Telly's phone before he could say anything. "Hello, Mom!"

"Hi Billy how are you doing? I'm so glad you called."

"I'm fine. I'm with Telly. Guess what? We spent the night in the truck, and we had a nice big breakfast. I had yummy pancakes with blueberries. Then we drove to another town to look around. It's called Blue. What's going on at the school?"

"Billy, we've had search parties and search dogs through the night and this morning. They've not found the kids yet. Some new people are here who said they are experts and could help us."

"Mom, I miss you. I hope someone finds them soon. I'm going to stay with Telly some more today." Billy handed the phone back to him.

Telly gave Billy's Mom a more complete update. She was still at the tent doing her best to cheer up the families and keep up their hopes. The search parties had continued all through the night and into the morning, and each time a search party came back, they were greeted by families eager for good news.

Chapter 15

Ami was back, looking a little more refreshed. She interviewed some of the newly arrived experts. The one standing closest to her was a grey-haired man with black-rimmed glasses. And he was wearing a lab coat. "Mr. Siebert, I understand you have a background in paranormal activity. Do you think what happened can be explained?"

"Well, I deal with the research end of it. I can't say at the moment that it can be explained in those terms. I've brought some equipment that I'm going to use to run some tests first."

"Thanks, Mr. Siebert. Please give me an update if you find something."

She also interviewed some conspiracy theorists. She turned to a man with tousled brown curly hair and deep frown marks on his forehead. "Mr. Randall, what do you think happened?"

"I think it's a conspiracy. It was set up this way, and they took the kids."

"Sir, who took the kids, and who is conspiring?"

"I think it's a group of people who do special missions. No one talks about them."

"Do you have anything to prove that what you are saying is true?"

"No, but I can tell you that it's a secret."

The reporter turned to a man in uniform and asked, "sheriff, do you have any answers?"

He shook his head. "I can't speculate at this time."

"I understand the State Police had been notified." Ami pursued her line of questioning, "So, do you have any information as to what happened?"

"We're still gathering information. At this time, we do not have conclusive information to offer the public. We are very much a part of the ongoing search. Until we have conclusive evidence, I'm not going to guess."

The reporter wrapped up this segment. "This is Ami Adams for WEXE. That's all for now."

Chapter 16

Telly asked Billy if he wanted to join the search party at the clearing. Billy was excited about it and eager to see the search dogs.

When they arrived, they saw a search party with about a dozen people and a couple of dogs spread out at the clearing and the area around it. Ray was in charge. He was delighted to see them and walked up to greet them. He smiled and looked at Billy. "We heard you found the watch, and then followed the shoe prints which led you here. We wouldn't be here if it wasn't for you, Billy!"

Billy looked pleased and mumbled. "I wanted to help."

Ray held out his hand and shook Billy's hand. Man to man. "Thank you."

One of the search dogs came closer to check out the new arrivals. Billy turned to pet him. "What's his name?"

"His name is Buddy. Would you like to go with Buddy for a bit?"

"Sure," Billy said. His face lit up. Buddy was already heading out. Turning quickly, he caught up with Buddy and his handler.

Ray said to Telly, "You were here last night and checked out the area?"

"Yes, it looks like the shoe prints came here and stopped." Telly pointed with emphasis. "They were walking in the same direction for awhile, then everyone stopped in this clearing and appeared to be facing there." He looked in that direction. "Have you found anything with the dogs?"

"The dogs confirm they were here where their shoe prints stopped. Of course it would help if they could tell us where those people went."

Telly nodded in agreement. "So what are you planning to do?"

"Right now we're gathering information and tagging all the spots that we had already covered. It may take awhile, but I want to be sure we cover all the areas."

"Well, if you need help, let me know."

"We're fine now. Thanks for offering."

"When Billy comes back, I'm going to head out with him and take another look at the next town."

Telly took off with Billy about an hour later. As they climbed back in the truck, Telly realized it was past 1 p.m. already, and they hadn't had lunch yet. He headed back with Billy to Big Bear where they had breakfast earlier. Telly ordered a burger and fries, and Billy ordered the same and a soda. The waitress remembered Telly from the morning, and said, "Hey hon, I've got a fresh pot of coffee brewing."

Telly nodded in appreciation. "Thanks, I need all the caffeine I can get." After the food arrived, they chomped on their burgers and fries.

Billy was looking thoughtful. All of a sudden, he asked, "Does this town have a school?" He missed his friends and even his teachers. He wanted to see the school here.

Telly turned to the waitress and asked her about the school. She said, "We have a very small school, it's the red brick building at the end of the street on the right."

Telly took a look at his watch. It was almost 2:15 p.m. "Billy, let's go now and see if we can make it there when the kids get out of school."

Billy brightened and sat up straighter. "OK, let's go."

Telly plunked some bills down on the table and added something extra for the tip. He sure appreciated the fresh coffee she brewed.

They headed out of the restaurant and drove toward the school. They had a few minutes to spare, so Telly parked in front. Soon the bell rang, the doors opened, and the kids rushed out. There was one school bus; a few kids boarded it, and it left. Telly sat and thought about the kids in his own town and how many times he had sat there and waited for them to come out of school to board his school bus. Telly wondered if he'd ever see those kids again. He felt a wave of sadness. The kids at this school will be going home where they live with their mothers, fathers, sisters, brothers, or grandparents. They would have a home to go to. Soon they would be having dinner at home, enjoying a home-cooked meal with their family. He could almost hear their laughter, the clinking of forks on plates at dinner and "Would you pass the butter?" "I'll have some more mac and cheese" "More mashed potatoes, please". He thought about the families in his town who didn't have dinner with their kids last night. No laughing, no arguing, no silliness. No reproaching looks from parents at the dinner table to quiet the kids down when they acted up. Instead, there would be just empty silence. Empty chairs, tables with no food, no sounds of talking, no laughter, no aroma of dinner cooking on the stove, no one at home, just an empty, silent house.

He looked over at Billy, and he saw a sad look on his face, too. Billy missed his friends, and the reality was setting in that they had not been found. They were still missing. Telly tried not to think of the unthinkable. He gave Billy a hug instead.

Chapter 17

B ack at the school, Billy's Mom was comforting Annie's Mom, who had been crying since she had heard the news. Her eyes were still red and puffy. She missed Annie so much. The routine of sending her off to school and watching for her to come home on the school bus played over and over in her mind like a videotape, each time sending waves of longing and sadness, bringing fresh tears at every wave. It was almost too much to bear. Annie's Dad was there to comfort her, but there wasn't much that he could do to stop the tears. He was restless and wanted to help. Anything was better than staying at the tent and doing nothing. He had signed up for a search party yesterday. He was gone for most of last night, then returned, and took a nap. He would be leaving again soon to go to the clearing site with another search party. He felt more useful doing something, yet he wished he could be there to comfort his wife. He missed Annie too but tried hard not to show it.

Liz's Mom and Annie's Mom spent a lot of time together at the tent talking and keeping each other company. Liz's Dad had also signed up for a search party and was gone for most of the night with Annie's Dad. They were neighbors and friends. They each in their way kept each other's spirits up and did what they could.

Bryan's Dad was a single parent. He had taken the news hard. Bryan was his only son. His Mom had passed away a few years ago. He was so proud of Bryan and how smart he was and how well he did in school. Bryan was a good kid who didn't cause him any problems. After his Mom died, Bryan took it hard and retreated into himself. He had always been closer to his Mom. She had practically raised him while his Dad went to work. But since his Mom passed, Bryan and his Dad had gotten a lot closer. It was natural that they turned to each other and that they sought comfort from each other. They were all the family that was left. Bryan was growing up fast. They treasured the time they spent together. His Dad made sure that his work didn't come between them and offered a lot of quality time to Bryan. Yesterday, when the kids disappeared, he was at work. When he heard the news, he immediately rushed to the school and took charge of the operations side and planning of the logistics. His background in engineering and project management came in handy.

Ron's parents came back to the school with Ron's little sister, Darla, after spending the night at their house last night. Darla was only 4 and didn't fully understand what was happening. She knew Ron was gone, and that something was up, perhaps something bad. Ron's parents tried to shield her from much of the turmoil, but there was no hiding the fact that the kids were missing. They reassured her by saying that people were looking for the missing kids, and they would be found soon. She seemed to be reassured that she would see Ron soon and occupied herself with her dolls, toys, and coloring books. Keeping her close by seemed to help Ron's parents. They took turns working at the volunteer tent, talking to the other parents, and helping to organize the search shifts. They stayed behind and kept busy.

The reporter Ami Adams was giving another update and talking about search parties and finding the shoe prints that led to the clearing. She had been interviewing members of search teams that had come back last night and today.

"Sir, have you found anything?" she asked a returning search-team volunteer.

"We spread out in the area from the school and used search dogs to help us."

"How far have you searched?"

"We've had several teams that expanded from here, going farther each time. We've also had a special dispatch with State Police who went to the site where it's presumed the shoe prints were last seen. We're going to cover the whole area and be sure we're not missing anything."

"Sounds like you are very well organized. We'll be back to get an update on the searches. Thank you."

Chapter 18

Telly asked Billy how he was doing. Billy shrugged and said he wanted to talk to his mother. Telly called Billy's Mom, "Hi. Billy wants to talk to you." He handed his phone to Billy.

Billy's Mom sounded tired. She was happy he called. "Billy how are you holding up?"

"Mom, I miss you. We're still looking for them. We don't know where they are."

"Billy, if you need anything, let me know. I love you."

"Ok, Mom, bye. Love you too."

Billy handed the phone back to Telly and sighed. "What do we do now?"

Telly started the truck and drove back to the new town, Blue, where they had gone earlier. Something had bothered him, and he wanted to take a second look. When they got there, he drove through and circled the town. It seemed that everyone was going about their business just like any other day. Nothing appeared out of the ordinary. Telly decided to drive a few miles out of town to see where it would take them. All of a sudden, he came upon a small airfield and some hangars. Somebody had spent good money to buy land and build this place. Why would they build this all the way out here, in the middle of nowhere? It didn't make any sense. He really wanted to know. The place was evidently private property, with "No Trespassing" signs prominently posted all around. The property was enclosed by a fence and gate. He wasn't about to break in and get into trouble. Telly drove around the complex and saw that it went further out than he expected. It was quite large, more than a mile. The buildings were all new, and the fence was also new. It was something he had not seen before or heard about. Telly wanted to know more and headed back to Blue to see what he could find out.

He drove to the only watering hole in town. It was after 4 p.m., and he could see quite a few guys in the bar already. He slid onto a stool and ordered a beer for himself and a soda for Billy. Billy wandered off to play one of the video games and left Telly by himself.

Telly nodded to the guy next to him, a stocky guy with thinning sandy hair "How's it going?" he asked.

The guy grunted.

"You just getting off work?"

The guy downed his beer before he answered. "Yeah."

"I'm new around here ... looking for work."

"You need to talk to the boss man if you're looking for work."

"Who is he? Where can I find him?"

"He's usually here at 5. He sits over there." The guy tilted his head toward a corner table in the back.

"What kind of work does he have? Construction? I noticed you've got quite a few new buildings and a new airport."

"You'll have to talk to him about that."

"OK, thanks, man."

Telly went to check on Billy. He was having a good time playing a war game, expertly maneuvering a machine gun. He had an absorbed look on his face and didn't want to be bothered at all.

Telly checked his watch and sat down at a table next to the corner table to wait for the boss man. He ordered some food for him and Billy and got something to drink while he was waiting. He thought about what he would say when the boss man came. He could honestly say he's looking for work and that he could do almost anything related to construction and carpentry. He had done a little bit of this and a little bit of that – roofing, electrical, plumbing, and even some masonry. He knew enough to get by and do a good job.

Telly looked up as a short balding man made his way to the corner table promptly at 5. He watched as the boss man took his seat, and the waitress immediately came over to take his order. She knew what he wanted; apparently he was a regular. Telly waited until he was settled, had his drink, and was waiting for his food. Then he leaned over and started a conversation.

"How do."

The boss man nodded back.

"I'm Telly and I'm in town with Billy". He pointed to where the boy was playing the video game. "They tell me you're the boss man. I'm looking for work."

"What kind of work do you do?"

"I do mostly construction and carpentry. I know a little about roofing, electrical, and plumbing, enough to make me dangerous." He smiled.

"We don't need anyone right now for that..." the boss man said, thinking. "But we could use some help with landscaping. Can you plant trees?"

"Sure – give me a shovel, and I can dig."

"All right can you work tomorrow? Be here at 6 a.m., and a truck will pick up the crew."

"I'll be here. Thanks."

Telly got Billy's food to go, then pulled a reluctant Billy away from his video game and told him they had to go home. Both he and Billy needed a change of clothes and a fresh shower. They've been away for only one day, but it seemed longer. Today was Tuesday.

Before they headed back to town, he called Billy's Mom and told her he was bringing Billy home. Billy didn't protest this time. When they arrived, she was waiting on the front porch. As soon as she saw them, she dashed out to meet them with arms outstretched. She gave Billy a big hug and kissed him on top of his head and his cheeks.

"Aw shucks, Mom." Billy managed to say as he wiggled away from her kisses.

"Am I glad to see you! If Telly kept you any longer, I would have come looking for you."

"Hey Mom, I was only gone since yesterday, you know. And I wanted to help."

"Billy's been the biggest help. He found the watch," Telly said proudly. "We weren't getting anywhere until

Billy found the watch. That led to the shoe prints and the clearing.”

“I was worried at first when you took him. I didn’t see any reason for Billy to go with you. But I know Billy wanted to be there, to help.”

“He’s a brave boy.”

“I know, and a part of me knew that it would be all right and that Billy had to do what he could to help. I’m so proud of him.”`

“I didn’t intend on keeping him for as long as I did, but it worked out.” Turning to Billy, Telly said, “Honestly, I was glad to have you with me.”

“And I like riding with Telly, and we sort of camped out under the stars.”

“Yeah, we did, and it sure was a beautiful night.” He hugged Billy and whispered something in his ear.

Holding his arm out, he gave her a handshake. “Thank you for letting me take Billy. What we went through together ... I’ll never forget it.” She squeezed his hand.

After leaving Billy’s house, Telly got in his pickup and drove straight to his place to shower and get a bite to eat. Then he called his sister. “Hey sis, how are you?”

“Telly, I was so worried. I hope they find those kids soon. How are you holding up?”

“Fine. I just got back in town with Billy. Have you heard anything new?”

“I haven’t heard anything. Let me know what you’re doing. Don’t let me worry.”

“Sure, sis. I’ve got some work lined up in the morning in Blue. I’ll probably work all day.”

"I didn't know there was work in that town. You do good, alright?"

"All righty, sis."

Next, he called Billy's Mom. "Hey, how's Billy doing?"

"Billy is fine," she said. "He just washed up. He's tired. I'm going to put him to bed to get some sleep." She paused. "I hear you were at Blue."

"Yep, we were there today. I'm headed back there in the morning. I'm going to check out a lead."

Chapter 19

WEDNESDAY

The alarm clock rang.

Telly opened his eyes slowly and peeked at the time. It was 3:30 a.m. *What day was this?* Telly slowly rolled out of bed, momentarily confused. Then he remembered what he doing today, that he was going to Blue.

He threw on a faded white t-shirt, ragged blue jeans, socks, and an old pair of sneakers. He made coffee and threw some eggs in the frying pan. He had some pancake batter left and poured some on the griddle as well. Soon the smell of breakfast and the coffee woke Telly up fully, and he ate heartily. He packed a couple of ham and cheese sandwiches for lunch, poured coffee in his travel mug, and grabbed his cap, work gloves, sunglasses, some bottled water and headed out.

The town Blue was quiet and sleepy when Telly got there. It was not quite 6 a.m. so he sat in his truck and waited in the parking lot of the bar. He saw three other guys loitering in front of the place. Soon a shiny new black truck came to pick up Telly and the other three guys. The driver motioned them towards the back. They climbed on, carefully stepping over the load of trees and shovels that filled the bed of the truck. They sat where they could fit in the spaces, with their legs scrunched up and bodies contorted.

The driver drove out of town towards the mini-airport hangar. He stopped at the gate, pressed a code, then drove in and followed along the fence line to where some trees had been freshly planted, with the soft dirt piled around the roots. He stopped the truck in front of the last tree. The crew sitting in the bed of the truck hopped out and unloaded the trees and the shovels from the back of the pickup truck. The driver drove away and disappeared after they unloaded the truck. Telly had started working right away and didn't notice where he went. It was still early; it felt great to be outdoors with the fresh coolness of the morning and a slight breeze. The crew of four worked well together. They paired up. One pair dug, and the other pair went down the line planting trees along the fence and filling the loose dirt back in the holes. Then they switched. It was mindless labor, and Telly easily fell into the rhythm of digging and planting on down the line. The other three guys didn't say much; apparently they all knew each other and had worked here before, probably had planted the other trees along the fence. He tried to start a conversation but wasn't very successful.

He glanced at his watch and saw that it was close to 11 a.m. As far as he could see, the closest building was about 100 yards from them. There was no sign of the black pickup, so Telly went back to work.

Not long after, the black truck showed up at the gate and came in to pick them up. It was lunchtime. The driver took them back to the bar and said he'd return in half an hour. Telly headed straight to the men's room. He washed up, splashed some cool water on his face, and ran his fingers over his hair. Telly ate the sandwiches that he had packed for his lunch and quickly swigged a cool beer. He was ready with the other three guys when the driver came back with the pickup truck loaded with more trees. The crew hopped on, sitting cramped and uncomfortable in the bed of the truck on the drive back. Then they got off, unloaded the trees and picked up right where they had left off.

Telly hadn't learned much of anything about the new place today. He had hoped they would be able to go in one of the buildings at the airport, but that didn't happen. He concentrated on the work. He tried to make conversation again with the crew, but they weren't interested. They didn't even talk much amongst themselves. Later in the afternoon, he heard the gate open. He looked up and saw a black van leaving. The windows were tinted, and he could not see much inside. Then another, and another black van passed by, three vans in total. They didn't look like work vans. They were shiny and new, just like the rest of the place. Telly went back to work, left in his own thoughts. He wondered where the vans were going.

Slowly, as the afternoon crawled by, he toiled under the sun. The sun was merciless. It got hotter and hotter. He was sweaty and dirty. His t-shirt was soaked and sticky. He couldn't wipe the sweat fast enough from his forehead, so he just let it drip. His arms, back ... his whole body ached from the grueling labor. Finally, at about 5 p.m., the driver showed up again with the pickup to take them back to the bar. He was relieved to see the truck. It had been an exhausting day. As the crew climbed off the bed of the truck, the driver peeled off some money and paid each of them in cash for their labor. Telly thought of asking him about work tomorrow but didn't say anything.

He decided he'd talk to the gas station attendant again on his way out of town. He pumped some gas and talked to the man, hoping to hear some good news. The radio was on at the gas station, and the reporter was giving an update. She covered the search teams' status and interviewed some more people. There wasn't any real news. The reporter sounded more tired than before – even discouraged.

Annie's Mom was on the air. She was pleading, "Please, if you know anything, please call the hotline number. If you have our kids, please return them. If it's ransom that you want, please tell us. We want our children back. Please call." The reporter repeated the hotline number after her plea, twice.

Chapter 20

Telly drove back to Rocky Flats, took a quick shower, put on a clean t-shirt and jeans, then headed to the school to see if he could help. The atmosphere had changed; there was an air of desperation. The search continued. The hotline was still getting calls, but some of the calls were really weird. The interviews were still being held in the tents, with more people being called in. By now all kinds of theories were being touted. There were people who were sure it was a UFO that came and sucked all the people up and carried them away. Others thought they simply evaporated into thin air. Some whispered that aliens had come to take them away for human food, and that the flesh of children was considered a delicacy. The rumors ran wild.

Telly saw Dottie at the volunteer station. She was in charge and busy with the incoming evening shift as the day shift was leaving. Dottie recognized him and waved him over. "Hi, Telly!"

Telly smiled broadly and walked over to give her a hug. He could tell she was in her element. She knew almost everyone and had a special knack of making them feel welcome and fitting them into volunteer slots that worked for their schedules and family situations. She kept volunteers coming back as repeats and wanting to help more, while rotating them on and off shifts around the clock. "You're doing a great job holding up the fort here, Dottie," Telly said. He signed up for a search team that started at 4 a.m. tomorrow. This would give him time to get dinner, grab some sleep and get back to the school.

"We've got so many people coming out to help; it's been so touching," Dottie said. "So many people care. They have come and joined the search parties, helped with the supplies, volunteered at the stations, brought home-cooked meals and stuff that we needed..."

"And the tents and stations were set up so quickly."

"Yeah, John was able to get that done first and got us the tents, equipment, table, chairs, blankets, cots, and quite a bit of the supplies."

"Yep, he's a mover and shaker."

Telly caught sight of Jen at the food and drink table. "Dottie, I'm going over to say hi to Jen before I head home. I'll be back here early in the morning to join the search party leaving at 4. I hope you get some rest."

Dottie smiled. "You get going then. We'll talk later." She gave Telly a hug.

Telly stopped to say hello to Jen. "Hi Jen, how's it going?"

Jen flashed him a quick smile, looking a bit disheveled with her long hair pulled back in a ponytail, a few loose hairs escaping here and there. "Telly, you're back! I heard Ray talking about Billy finding the watch and how you guys tracked the shoe prints to the large clearing among rocks." Jen talked and gestured exuberantly.

"Billy's sharp eyes caught the glint of the watch," Telly said proudly. "We were just driving on the road ... we really lucked out." He paused. "Ray was leading that search team when Billy and I saw and talked to him. They were searching that area with the dogs."

"Are you going out again?"

"I'll be back here at 4 in the morning ... heading out with a search party."

"Ray said he's also going out at 4 tomorrow. He just got back and went home to get some shut-eye before he leaves again in a few hours."

"I'll be with him tomorrow. Listen, you get some rest too, OK? I'll see you later."

"Bye, Telly. Good luck tomorrow." Jen gave him a quick hug.

"Thanks, Jen." Telly grinned at her and walked toward his pickup.

He drove back to his place and made four thick ham and cheese sandwiches, two to eat now, and two to take with him early in the morning. Telly set his alarm for 3 a.m. He turned off the night lamp and went to bed, but tossed and turned, trying to sleep. His mind was racing with all kinds of thoughts about the missing kids. He felt anxious about tomorrow. He was restless. He teetered in that no-man's-land, in the space between awake and sleep, where he wandered like a lost soul, caught between two worlds. It was a long time before Telly finally drifted off to sleep.

Chapter 21

THURSDAY

His alarm went off at 3 a.m. Telly quickly got his things together for the early-morning search team. He ate a cold breakfast of cereal and milk, gulped down some coffee, put the rest in his mug, and grabbed his sandwiches and an apple to go. Telly got to the school a few minutes early and talked to Ray, who was leading this search, to find out where they were going. Ray was looking at the map and wanted to go farther out from where they had searched before in the clearing areas. Today the plan was to start at an area at the base of the mountain. The search team got into their trucks and headed out, following Ray's truck. They were ready and eager to go.

They stopped at the edge of the tree-covered area at the base of the mountain. Telly got out of his truck and checked his equipment. The search team gathered around Ray as he gave them maps and instructions.

Each pair had an area to cover. Telly ended up teamed with Ray, and they headed out together on foot towards the trees to start their methodical search. They soon reached the trees and set out on a trail that led to the camping areas, walking up a slight incline. They made good progress. The first camping area was deserted. The forest was quiet as they proceeded. The day was breaking, and they worked efficiently as a team, covering the area thoroughly. The terrain was only slightly sloped, and they didn't encounter any problems. It took them a couple of hours to cover their territory, from the base of the mountain. As they headed back down toward the trucks to meet up with the others, it was daylight.

They discussed where to go next. Ray studied the map then pointed his finger at the lake. It was not too far from where they were. The search team headed out in their trucks.

Chapter 22

The lake was on flat land in a quiet, secluded area. They parked, got out of their trucks, and surveyed the lake. It was tranquil and calm, with barely a ripple. Ray wanted to check it out. If anything had been dumped into the lake, they would have to get divers and special equipment to do the search. They walked closer to the lake and looked around, seeing nothing out of the ordinary. Nevertheless, Ray made a note to get some divers to the lake tomorrow. It would take some planning to get the gear and divers, and he'd have to contact the feds or state to coordinate it.

The dogs had been quiet until they got to the lake. As they slowly made their way around to the other side of the lake, the dogs started to bark and jump in excitement. The search party quickened its pace to keep up with the dogs pulling on the leashes. The dogs led the way toward a cabin. It was sort of run-down and apparently in disuse. But the dogs kept barking louder. Ray tried the door. The doorknob was a bit rusty and didn't quite fit. He turned the knob. It was not locked. It was dark inside the cabin, so Ray flicked on his flashlight and carefully made his way in. There was no one in the first room. The dogs headed toward a back room, tails wagging fast with excitement.

There was another door. Telly turned the doorknob and tugged at it. The door appeared to be stuck. He pushed a little harder and thought he heard a soft muffled moan. He signaled to the search team as they crept up behind him and held up his hand for them to stay put, to keep back. He slowly wedged his left arm and shoulder through the door, shined his flashlight, and peeked inside.

He gasped. The room was full of the missing kids and adults, all lying down and not moving. His heart stopped still. They can't all be dead! Very slowly, Telly slid into the room while keeping the door cracked open. He bent down and checked the first person, lying face-down behind the door. There was a pulse! Telly gently pulled the child from behind the door, widened the doorway, and gestured for Ray to hold the boy under the arms. Together, they pulled the first child carefully out the door, carried him to the front room, and laid him on the floor. Telly took a closer look at him and recognized who it was – Bryan! The search team worked quickly, and carefully carried more people out to the first room while making room and spreading out the rest of the people in the back room. They counted everyone, 28 in all ... 25 students and 3 teachers. All the missing students and teachers were there and accounted for! They quickly checked each one to see if there was a pulse. Telly looked for Annie, Liz, and Ron's familiar faces and found them. He felt their pulses and bent down to watch them breathe. They were all alive! Telly felt a jolt of joy and said a silent prayer of thanks. He had no idea what had happened to them or why they were not awake, but they were alive, along with the others. A brief thought crossed his mind that they might have been drugged or something.

Ray tried to call, but there was no cell reception in this area. So he decided to make a run back to Big Bear to call for backup and ambulances. The rest of the search team stayed with Telly. They did what they could to make everyone more comfortable; straightened out legs and arms and rested heads on blankets or folded pieces of clothing. The people had not awakened, and Telly wanted to be there when they did. From what he remembered about the kids on his bus, it looked like they still had on the same clothes. They were just disheveled. Telly didn't know what to make of it. He was so glad they were alive but puzzled that they were in this state. Will they snap out of it soon?

After some time, Telly heard the sound of vehicles approaching. Ray was back with an ambulance, a limo and four vans. The search team quickly helped the medic, and the drivers put the kids on stretchers. They carried out the smallest kids first, filling up the ambulance, then the limo and the vans. The plan was to drop off the kids in this group first, then come back for the bigger kids and the adults. After they left, Telly went to check on the rest. Telly noticed that Ron was still in the room. He was one of the bigger kids who would be picked up at the next trip with the three adults. Telly checked his pulse again and saw that he was breathing restfully. After a while, Ron stirred. Telly gently touched him. Ron responded, as his eyelids trembled and fluttered open. He blinked slowly, then more rapidly, in an attempt to clear his sight. He looked around and turned his head to focus his eyes on Telly. As a glow of recognition lit up in his eyes, Telly touched Ron's arm lightly and said "Ron, you're OK now. We found you and everyone at the school."

Ron tried to speak. "Whh ... what ... where am I?"

Telly said, "Ron, you're safe. We found you ... and everyone."

Ron was still trying to speak and looked confused. "Where ... am I?"

"You're at a cabin by the lake."

"How ... did ... I get here?" Ron stammered.

"We don't know. You disappeared after school on Monday. The whole school went missing expect for Billy who hid in a cabinet until I found him. He was safe and sound. We sent out search parties and ended up finding everyone here."

"What...?"

"Ron, I just want to make sure you're alive and well. Are you hurting anywhere? How are you feeling?"

"I feel a little groggy and stiff. I think ... I'm fine. I'm not hurting anywhere."

"Good, just get some rest now. Let me know if you need anything."

Ron closed his eyes and rested his head, as Telly adjusted some blankets to make him more comfortable.

Telly heard the sound of vehicles returning. He helped the returning medic and search-team volunteers carry the rest of the people out of the cabin. As the last person was carried out and put in a vehicle, Telly jumped in his truck and headed back to Rocky Flats with the caravan.

Chapter 23

As soon as he got cell-phone service, Telly called Annie's Mom and told her everyone had been found and rescued. Annie's Mom was at the school when the news broke about the rescue. She told Telly that all the parents had rushed to the clinic when they heard the children were being taken there, including Liz's parents, Bryan's Dad, and Ron's parents and his little sister. Everyone was excited, some cried with joy on the safe return of their children as they reunited with them, others danced in celebration. Billy had come back to the school with his Mom, and they took off to the clinic to visit his classmates as soon as they heard the news.

Ami was on air, jubilantly reporting that the 25 children and the three teachers had all been found alive. People were jumping with joy, hugging each other, laughing in relief, and celebrating the good news. Everyone was talking at once about the safe return of the missing 28. The reporter interviewed the people who had predicted their safe return. They were all quick to say on air that this was exactly what they had predicted, that all would be found safe and no harm would come to them.

As the children were being taken to the clinic to be checked out before being released to their parents, and tents with makeshift cots were being set up outside the clinic to accommodate the overflow of kids and the three teachers, Telly first stopped by the school. He caught sight of Ray as he was talking to Jen at the school. Ray looked exhausted but happy.

"Hey Ray, how much sleep have you had?"

"Not much ... I couldn't get really rested until I knew we've found them."

"You're going to catch up on your sleep now?"

"Yep, I'm going back to crash at my place. I'm too tired to do anything else."

"So much has happened. We were lucky to have found them."

"I try not to think about what could have happened otherwise," said Ray with a sigh.

"I thought the dogs were barking up the wrong tree, the way they were acting."

"They were sure right about where they were going."

"I need to let you go so you can get some rest."

"See you later and hey... thanks for your help today," hollered Ray on his way out.

Telly turned to Ray's sister Jen. She had been there throughout the ordeal, working at the food and drink tent and serving volunteers and parents throughout this time. She threw him a cheerful smile.

Telly felt great. "Hi Jen!"

She came over and gave him a hug. "Hi yourself."

"Have you been here all this time?"

"Yeah ... I've stayed here and camped out on the cot over there." Jen inclined her head towards the tent with the cots.

"You've been on your feet and working hard." Telly paused. "Would you like to go sit and have a bite to eat at the diner?"

She grinned. "I'd love that. I'm starved and a fresh cup of coffee would be great!"

"Let's go ... we'll hop in my truck."

Jen hadn't had lunch. Inside the restaurant, the smell of food triggered her hunger pangs and her stomach started to grumble. The waitress brought coffee quickly. It was comforting to sip the warm coffee ... so good. She ordered poached eggs, toast, and some fruit.

The waitress placed their orders, and their food came quickly.

"Want some bacon?" Telly had ordered eggs, bacon and waffles.

"No thanks, I don't eat meat."

"You're a vegetarian?"

"I still eat eggs. I've cut out the meat. I don't even miss it."

"Health reasons?" Telly inquired.

"It was an ethical decision for me. And it is healthier."

"How did you come to that decision? If you don't mind telling me, I'd like to know."

"I became aware of the environmental effects of factory farming when I did a research project for my class in college. But it didn't translate into a personal decision until later." Jen paused to reflect. Telly nodded and re-filled her coffee cup. "Several months later, as I was driving on the highway, I saw a vehicle hauling a trailer packed with animals on their way to slaughter. It was their last ride." Jen looked into Telly's eyes. "That was the moment it became real for me. I made up my mind to become a vegetarian – right then and there."

"I respect your decision, and I know this is important to you," Telly said this slowly, with newfound pride and respect. "I'm very glad you shared this with me."

"It was what I had to do." They sat in comfortable silence for a while.

Telly inclined his head towards the floor. "So, how're your feet? You must be tired after being on your feet for so long."

She shrugged her shoulders. "I'm feeling much better and relaxed now."

Telly filled her in on the activities of the search team and emphasized the critical role that Billy played in finding the kids. "If Billy hadn't found the watch, there's no telling what might've happened."

"I heard about that from Ray. Finding the watch led to finding the kids. That was amazing!"

"Billy is a smart and brave kid, and he's a survivor."

"I just could not imagine what if..." She looked at him intensely, not wanting to speak the unimaginable. "It was a miracle that everyone was found safe." Jen described what happened in town. "In the excitement of it all, no one talked about what might have happened in the last few days ... where did they go and what happened to them."

"I wondered about that myself," Telly said. "I'm so glad they are alive, and apparently well. I talked to Ron, one of the kids that ride my bus. He said he wasn't hurt, and appeared to be fine, except for being a little groggy."

"Did he tell you where he went?" Jen asked, shifting her body forward to catch his answer.

"No, I don't think he knew, or he would have said something. If anyone had been missing, we would have continued searching for them. But everyone was found and accounted for. So we stopped the search."

"Do you think they were at the cabin the whole time?"

"I honestly don't know. I'm just glad we found them alive. When we first went to the lake, we were planning to get a diving team out there to search in the lake and look for them. I'm glad we found them in the cabin and didn't have to dive in the lake."

"It's a miracle."

Telly smiled and took a nice long sip of his coffee. It was strong and so good. Hey – and the company wasn't bad either. Jen sat back and relaxed her shoulders into the curve of the booth. She slipped her shoes off, and wiggled, stretched and curled her toes underneath the table.

They sat and talked, took their time slowly with their meal and savored every bite. They were both hungry but didn't want to rush. There was no need to. The waitress put a new pot of coffee on the table and left them alone. Telly kept Jen's cup refilled.

Chapter 24

The clinic was packed with the kids and their families. Inside, stretchers lined the hallways and every room was filled. Starting with the smallest children first, the doctor and nurse were checking each kid and running tests. By now most of the kids had awakened but a few were still a little groggy. The clinic staff processed the kids as quickly as they could, one by one, doing the checks on all of them. As they finished with one person, they quickly moved on to the next, carefully going through each room.

When the tests came back on the first kids that had arrived, the doctor looked over the results to decide what to do. So far all the children checked out fine, so they wouldn't have to stay overnight at the clinic. There wasn't enough room for everyone anyway. The staff was relieved that the results were coming back normal. The doctor made his way around the small clinic. He talked to the parents and gently let them know that their children would need to stay at the clinic until all checks were completed and the results came back. If they didn't find anything wrong, the patients would be released one by one. If anyone needed more medical care, they would be transported to the county hospital in Valley City. The parents remained by their children's side and watched them closely, hoping that soon they would all be going home.

Annie's Mom held Annie's hand as she slowly woke up. She was the first person Annie saw when she opened her eyes. Annie smiled as her Mom leaned down to kiss Annie. *Boy, was she glad to see her Mom!*

"How are you feeling? Are you hurting anywhere?"

Annie shook her head. "I just feel ... a little sleepy. I'm ... not ... hurting anywhere."

Annie's Mom squeezed her hand. "I love you so much."

"Mom ... I know that. I love ... you ... too."

They smiled and hugged each other. Annie's Mom gave her another long hug, as if she couldn't get enough of Annie and wanted to be sure she was there, all there.

Annie looked around. "Where ... am I?"

"You are at the clinic."

"Where is ... everyone? Are they all safe?'

"Yes, everyone is safe and sound." Annie's Mom smiled. "They're all in the clinic or the tents outside."

Annie sighed. Her Mom kissed her on her forehead softly. "You get some rest. I'll be right here. I'm not going away. The doctors will be coming by soon to check you out, and then we can all go home."

In the next room, Bryan's eyes slowly fluttered open. He saw his Dad at his side, "Dad..."

"Bryan! You're awake." He squeezed Bryan's hand.

"Dad ... where am I?"

"You're at the clinic."

"What ... happened, Dad?"

"Bryan, everyone at the school went missing except for Billy who crawled in a cabinet, and hid there until Telly found him. We don't know what happened."

"Where ... is everyone?"

"Everyone is here, safe, at the clinic."

"Dad, I'm ... so glad ... to see you. I ... love you." Bryan held on to his Dad's hand, not ready to release it yet.

"Bryan, you know I love you. I just don't say it as much as I should. You are all that I have..." His voice shook a little and he wet his lips before he continued. "I wish your Mom could see you now. I know she's with us. I'm so glad to have you back safely."

"Me too."

"I'll be here. I'm not going to leave your side."

"I know, Dad. I know."

Telly came back to the clinic and made his rounds. He talked to Bryan and his father, Annie and her parents, Ron and his parents and little sister, too. Ron's family didn't want to leave Ron, so they brought Darla. She carried her favorite rag doll. Billy and his Mom were also at the clinic, visiting his friends and their families. In the midst of all the activity, Billy's role in finding them was forgotten and no one spoke of it.

The rooms were filled with soft sighs of relief and hurried whispers as words tumbled out. Tears flowed as easily as cries of joy when people found their loved ones. The families were all rejoicing, touching, holding, talking, and laughing; all the while driving away the last traces of despair, anguish, and worry.

Telly was exhausted, but it didn't matter. At the same time, he felt more energetic and alive than he had for a long time. He was going to sleep well tonight. By now it was almost 8 p.m. The doctor finally started to release the patients, one by one. All the children had passed the final checks, so they were released and went home with their joyful and very tired parents. Telly stayed until the last child was released. He was relieved when he heard that Rocky Flats Elementary School would be closed tomorrow, Friday.

Telly went back to his place and set his alarm for 8 a.m. the next day since school was cancelled. Something was bothering him, though, and he couldn't quite put his finger on it ... but he was so tired. As soon as Telly's head hit the pillow, he fell asleep immediately. He dreamt of endless footprints, the moonlight, the clearing surrounded by rocks, fire pits in the woods, the faces of the children dancing by, the lake and the cabin, the trees he planted, the strange shining new buildings ... all these images were floating by in his dream blending and fading and coming back across his vision, mixing with each other then separating and reappearing together at some point. Finally, the alarm broke through his restless sleep. He shut out the night, pushed it away and closed that door in his mind. He woke up to a new day.

Chapter 25

FRIDAY

Telly welcomed the sun, watching its rays shining brightly through the sheer curtains. It was morning and another beautiful day. He lingered in bed just a bit, enjoying the moment.

He dressed quickly, pulling on a clean white t-shirt, socks, and a pair of faded jeans. He wasn't hungry. He rushed out, got in his truck and started driving, not really thinking about where he was going but just driving. Before he realized it, Telly was heading towards Blue. He drove straight into town to the bar, then got out of his truck and went inside. It was mid-morning, and business was slow. He and the bartender were the only two there. Telly sat at the bar and ordered a beer. The bartender was a beefy looking guy, with curly brown hair on the outskirts of a receding hairline. Telly started the conversation. "Have you heard the news? All the missing kids from the Rocky Flats School have been found."

The bartender looked at him. "Yep, that was all over the news. I heard the search party found them in a cabin by the lake."

"Are you from around these parts?"

"I've been here a year or so. How about you?"

"I'm from Rocky Flats where the school kids went missing. I was born and raised there."

"You came here for a reason?"

"Well, I'm wondering if you can tell me about the mini-airport a few miles outside of town. It's new and the buildings are new. Do you know who owns them?"

"Why do you want to know?"

"Well something doesn't seem right." He looked at the bartender, sensing a bit of cool reserve. "I mean ... why build fancy new buildings out here in the middle of nowhere? I figure someone's either trying to hide something, or there's something weird going on."

"I don't get a lot of strangers coming in asking questions. Why are you asking?"

"I think there's a connection between that place and the missing children. I can't put my finger on it, but something bothers me."

"Well I don't see what you are driving at. You think someone here is involved with the missing children?" The bartender was staring intently at Telly now.

"That's my theory."

"Do you have any proof, or are you just coming in here fishing?"

"Tell you the truth, I was hoping you could help me out."

"You think I could tell you something?" he asked. "You want another beer?"

"Yeah ... I guess so. Let me have another one." The bartender got Telly another bottle, popped the cap, and handed it to him. Then he walked behind the counter and through the curtains into a backroom of the bar.

Telly nursed his beer, chiding himself for asking questions that now sounded somewhat foolish in broad daylight. His phone rang, and he looked at the number and answered. "Oh, hi sis."

"Hi Telly. I heard the good news. I'm so glad and relieved you found the kids. The reporter Ami Adams is on the radio now. She said they are disassembling the tents, and a lot of people are helping to pack up the stuff. She's announced earlier that the children have the day off. There's no school today. School will re-open on Monday. What are you doing now?"

"I'm in Blue. I took a drive back out here this morning."

"I'm hoping you could stop by this Sunday for dinner. We didn't get a chance to get together last week."

"Well, it's been quite a week. School is still closed, so I'm actually taking today off. I promise I'll make it to Sunday dinner this time. What are we having?"

"Your favorite foods. It'll be special. Bring someone if you like."

"Yum, I'll be there. I may bring someone this time."

"Hmm ... who is it?"

"Bye, sis." Telly laughed and ended the call.

He dialed Jen's number. "Hi, good morning."

"Hi yourself, did you sleep well last night?" Jen asked.

"Not as well as I would have liked to. I was tired and fell into a deep sleep, but during the night I tossed and turned. I don't know, something was bothering me, something didn't feel right. How about you, did you sleep well?"

"Did I ever! I was exhausted."

"Hey, my sister is cooking dinner Sunday night, and she said to come and bring someone," Telly said. Then he stopped to take a breath. "So ... I was hoping you could come. Maybe ... if you are ... I mean ... are you free Sunday night?" He wanted to sound casual, not make a big deal out of it. But it was. It would be the first time he'd be bringing a girl home to his sister's for Sunday dinner.

"Well, as a matter of fact I am free," Jen said warmly. "I'd love to go!"

"Oh great, I'll pick you up at 6 p.m." Telly was delighted and relieved.

"OK ... so what are you up to today? I heard school was out."

"I'm at Blue. I came across this town the other day when Billy and I were searching for the children. Have you ever been here?"

"No, tell me what it looks like."

"Well it's a small town, like ours. But they've got some new buildings and even a small airfield and hangar, like a mini-airport, outside of town."

"I haven't been there. Where exactly is this?"

"Well you know where Big Bear is? This town is less than an hour from there, if you're heading northeast."

"So you're just hanging out or what?"

"As matter of fact, I was just talking to the bartender here, trying to find out what the deal is with the new airfield and the new buildings in town. He doesn't seem to know anything about it."

"Maybe he doesn't, but ... usually the bartender knows everything, especially in a small town. Did you tell him why you're asking?"

"Yep, I told him something didn't feel right, and I thought there was a connection between the missing school children and that place."

"That's interesting. What did he say to that?"

"He didn't exactly say. I may be barking up the wrong tree. I think I'll just finish my beer and head out."

Telly hung up his phone and finished the last of his beer. He looked around the empty place. The bartender was not back yet. He was still the only customer. Telly got up from his barstool, put some money down, and headed toward the door.

He opened it and hesitated a moment for his eyes to adjust. Going from the dark watering hole to the bright sunlight temporarily blinded him. He felt something then tumbled into total darkness.

Chapter 26

Telly woke up on a table, a stainless steel one. A single light was shining in the room. He was disoriented and couldn't remember what had happened. He didn't know where he was, and then it slowly came to him. The last thing he remembered was getting up from his barstool at the watering hole and going to the door. That was it. He looked around the room. It was sterile and white. He looked down at his arms and realized that he was strapped to the table.

What the heck? Where am I ... what's happening?

He looked around the room again, slowly. This time he noticed a small camera mounted high on the wall. It was aimed straight at him. He watched as the red light on the camera flickered and blinked. He felt a chill. A voice said, "Mr. Terrance O'Brian?" It sounded vaguely familiar.

Telly froze. "Who ... who are you? How do you know my name? Why am I here?"

"Mr. Terrance O'Brian. We know who you are. Tell us what you are doing here."

The new guy that came into town a week ago, last Friday! It freaking sounded like Steve!

"Steve?" Telly cried out.

Chapter 27

Suddenly a blinding light shone directly in Telly's eyes. He blinked and turned his head away from the light. "Steve, is that you?"

"Let me ask the questions, Mr. O'Brian. I will tell you this. You are in the new building at the airport. Why did you come back to Blue?"

"I saw the new buildings, and ... I was curious ... wanted to see what was happening here."

"You were here three times before. Why did you come back again today?"

"Ahh ... I was just curious."

"You will answer truthfully and completely."

Telly kept his mouth shut this time. All of a sudden the room went dark, as all the lights went out. Then he heard a noise, a door opening. Telly felt something cool touch him, then a mask was placed over his eyes. The door closed, and he heard another voice, a deep one this time. "Think of something in your past ... you are going to go back, way back to when you were a child ... think of your first memories of your mother ... your father." The voice droned on and on. Telly realized he was starting to fall into a hypnotic state. He tried to stay awake, but the voice droned on and on. Telly tried to resist. He focused on a splinter in his hand that he got on the day he was planting trees. He focused on the pain and tried to block out the droning voice as much as he could. The voice went on and on. He magnified the pain in his mind until it surpassed the voice and blocked it out.

Finally the droning voice stopped. He heard the first voice, Steve's voice, say, "We are peaceful." Then, gently this time, he asked, "Why did you come back?"

Telly decided to answer truthfully. "I think there is a connection between this place and the missing children. I think they were kidnapped from the school and brought here for some reason. I want to know ... did you bring them here? Did you hurt them?"

"We do not hurt children. We took the children. No harm was done to them."

"But why ... why did you take the children?"

"We believe children are the future. We are alarmed at children killing children, in school shootings. Children killing themselves." Steve paused. "We have developed a new technology. We believe it is accurate more than 90% of the time. We can now identify those children who have violent tendencies."

"You are using our children as guinea pigs?"

"For the greater good. The children are not harmed."

"Why us? Why our children?"

"These children are in a small town, in a rural and somewhat isolated area. They have not been exposed to all the violence in the outside world."

"What happened to them?"

"We have not harmed them. After we identified the children who have violent tendencies, we separated them from the others and put them into a trance. We inserted a subliminal message that will counteract any violence that may be acted out in the future. Each time before any violent act occurs, the subliminal message will be triggered. The children will not remember anything. No one would be hurt."

"Why am I here?"

"You were seeking answers. You wanted to know. You are here because we want you to have the answers." He paused then continued. "We know you care about the children. The children with violent tendencies will not ever become violent. They will not hurt other children, themselves, or any other people or animals. They will grow up and live peacefully as adults. We will have a peaceful world. Imagine a world without crime. A world without wars. Humankind will finally live together in peace. These children will be the children of the future. Mr. O'Brian, do you understand?"

"I ... understand. You mean the children no harm."

"Mr. O'Brian. You will be put into a deep trance. When you awake you will not remember anything, but you will be at peace."

This time the droning voice came back, and Telly did not fight it. He drifted off and finally went to a place, a deep place.

Chapter 28

Telly woke up in his truck outside the watering hole. He thought he must have dozed off. He could not remember why he was here, except to get a beer. He felt satisfied, somehow, so he started up his truck and headed home.

Telly drove leisurely. It was a beautiful day. The world seemed brighter, a better place. It had been quite a week, one that he'd never forget. Now that everything was back to the way it had been, he was looking forward to Sunday dinner at his sister's and seeing Jen again. He made a mental note to call his sister to tell her that Jen was a vegetarian. Who knows, maybe he would ease off the meat himself. He smiled thinking of her.

Telly was happy. He didn't know why he felt that way, he just did. But then again, there was something, something else he couldn't quite wrap his mind around. He shivered as a cold chill ran through his body. He shook his head; there's no use worrying about something that hasn't happened yet. Better to just enjoy the day than to worry about the future.

Chapter 29

It was still early in the afternoon when Telly got back into town. There was plenty of time to check on the kids on his bus route since school was closed today. He didn't want to wait until Monday.

He stopped by Bryan's house. Bryan was home with his Dad. He looked rested and back to normal. "Hey, Bryan, how's it going?"

"Great. How about you, Telly?"

Telly grinned. "As good as it gets."

"I took the day off from work," Bryan's Dad said. "We're spending some special father and son time together this weekend." He paused. "We've lots to catch up on." He reached out and gave Bryan's shoulder a warm, firm squeeze. They both smiled.

"I'm glad to hear that. You've both been through a lot." Telly turned to leave.

"Thanks for stopping by, Telly."

"No problem." He looked at Bryan. "See you Monday morning, bright and early."

Chapter 30

Telly drove down the road to Annie's house. Annie opened the door at the first knock, "Hey, Telly!"

"I see you are back to your usual self."

"Yup."

"Annie got a good night's rest last night," her Mom said. "And she's happy there's no school today."

Annie beamed and nodded.

Telly just grinned.

Annie's Mom added, "Listen, I never got the chance to thank you ... for all you've done. I know how much you care about these kids."

"I'm just glad they're all safe and sound," Telly said.

She turned towards the kitchen, from which wonderful smells were emanating. "Would you like some home-baked cookies? We started making them this morning."

Telly's eyes widened in delight as he followed her to the kitchen and saw the cookies.

"We've got chocolate chip cookies here and peanut-butter cookies in the trays over there." She pointed to another tray on the countertop. "Annie and I just finished frosting those sugar cookies. Would you like to try some?"

Telly looked down at the cookies trying to decide. "Don't mind if I do. Hmm ... chocolate chip ... mmm ... these are one of my favorites!" He stuffed one in his mouth.

"Have some more ... here put them on this plate. We'll be baking more today. It's fun for us." She started laughing. "Annie and I were just talking about starting our own cookie business..."

"Annie and Mom's Cookies," Annie blurted out.

"Right. Just so you know, Annie came up with the name."

"I like it," Telly said as he nodded in agreement. He made his way to the door carrying the plateful of cookies in his hand. Annie and her Mom walked behind him, looking pleased.

"I'm going to enjoy these special cookies. Thanks!" He turned to say goodbye. "I'll be seeing you and Annie bright and early Monday morning."

They smiled and waved.

Chapter 31

Next, Telly headed down the road to see Liz. He had not talked to her at the clinic and was looking forward to seeing her. Liz was home when he knocked. She opened the door and jumped up and down when she saw him. "Telly!" She turned to her parents sitting on the living room couch. "It's Telly. Telly's here!"

It was apparent that Liz's parents had both taken the day off to be with her. "I just want to stop by and see how Liz is doing. I didn't get a chance to talk to her yesterday." He directed his gaze at Liz and looked at her carefully. "How are you, Liz?"

"Good as new. I think I'm better than ever," Liz said. Her parents chuckled.

"I'm glad to hear that."

Liz piped up. "I'm bored. I want to go somewhere and do something fun. But my parents are babysitting me like I'm recovering from some illness ... ugh. But I feel fine."

"You look fine to me, Liz."

Liz's parents laughed. "You can tell she's back to her old self. She's probably got more energy now than ever," her Mom said.

"We're just trying to decide what to do next," her Dad added. "I think we'll go outside and play ball, get some of this energy out."

"We appreciate what you did to get her back to us," her Mom said.

Telly fidgeted, shy with compliments. He turned to leave.

"We're going out for dinner at the restaurant to celebrate Liz's homecoming." She paused. "...and we're going to go shopping. Somehow Liz has lost her new watch."

Chapter 32

Telly got in his truck and headed down the road to Ron's house. He saw Ron in the front yard playing ball with his little sister, Darla. They were both laughing and jumping to throw and catch the ball. Ron's Mom was looking out the window. She smiled and waved when she saw Telly.

Telly waved back. "Hey Ron, take care of that little sister of yours, OK?"

"You betcha!" Ron hollered, holding the ball in his hands. "Know what? I really missed Darla. And ... Mom and Dad of course."

"Listen, I'm glad you're having fun with your sister. I don't want to hold you up. I'll see you on Monday, bright and early."

Chapter 33

Telly's last stop was to see Billy. His Mom answered the door. "Hi, Telly!"

"Hi, how's Billy doing?"

"Oh he's doing great. He's out in the back yard."

"I just saw Bryan, Annie, Liz and Ron. They're enjoying the day off from school. Everyone is fine."

"I'm glad to hear that. I want to thank you for bringing Billy back safely through all of this."

"That's the least I can do. Billy is a good kid, and he's smart."

"And thank you for finding him at the school, cramped in the cabinet. This is one time I'm glad he's smaller than the other kids." She sighed and shook her head. "I used to get so upset when some of the bigger kids were picking on him. I prayed that he would grow bigger – faster."

"I know," Telly said. "I've seen him in the school yard. The bigger kids sometimes give him a hard time, I mean, not the kids on the bus, but some of the other kids at school. He keeps it to himself, doesn't like to talk about it."

"Well I'm teaching him to defend himself. He's getting quite good," she said.

"Really?"

"Why don't you go see for yourself. He's target practicing in the back yard."